To Mark, Wendy, Glenn, and Larry with love—
and to the new love of my life, Jacob Douglas—C.R.

To my parents—V.G.

First published in the United States, Great Britain, Canada, Australia, and New Zealand in 1999
by NorthSouth Books Inc., an imprint of NordSüd Verlag AG, CH-8005 Zürich, Switzerland.

Hardcover edition published in 2013 by NorthSouth Books.
Distributed in the United States by NorthSouth Books Inc., New York 10016.

A CIP catalogue record for this book is available from The British Library.
Library of Congress Cataloging-in-Publication Data
Roth, Carol.
Little Bunny's Sleepless Night / Carol Roth; illustrated by Valeri Gorbachev.
p.   cm.
Summary: Little Bunny, an only child, is so lonely that he cannot sleep, so he asks
his friends Squirrel, Skunk, Porcupine, Bear, and Owl if he can stay with them,
only to discover that his own bed is best.
[1. Bedtime–Fiction. 2. Sleep–Fiction. 3. Only child–Fiction.
4. Rabbits–Fiction. 5. Animals–Fiction.]
I. Gorbachev, Valeri, ill. II. Title.
PZ7.R727421   1999 [E–dc21] 98-43047

The artwork consists of pen-and-ink watercolor.

ISBN: 978-0-7358-4123-9
Printed in China by Leo Paper Products Ltd., Heshan, Guangdong, January 2013.
1   3   5   7   9   •   10   8   6   4   2
www.northsouth.com

Little Bunny's Sleepless Night

by **Carol Roth** · illustrated by **Valeri Gorbachev**

North
South

Little Bunny had no brothers or sisters. He had his very own room with his very own bed.

But sometimes he got lonely—so lonely that he couldn't fall asleep.

One night he thought: What I need is the company of a good friend.

So he hopped next door to his good friend
Squirrel. "May I sleep here tonight?"

"Of course," said Squirrel as he welcomed him in.
Tucked all snug in bed next to Squirrel, Little Bunny
thought how lucky he was not to be alone.

"Good night, Squirrel," said Little Bunny.

"Good night, Little Bunny," answered his friend.

Falling asleep was easy, but staying asleep was not.
Little Bunny was soon awakened by *CRUNCH, CRUNCH, CRUNCH!*
"What's that noise?" he asked as he sat up in bed.
"It's just me cracking acorns," said Squirrel. "I always have
a little snack in the middle of the night."
"Well, thanks for having me, but I can't sleep with all that noise!"

So Little Bunny left and hopped some more until he reached his good friend Skunk.

"May I sleep here tonight?"

"YES! YES! A HUNDRED TIMES YES!" shouted Skunk. "No one has ever asked to sleep over before!"

Afraid Little Bunny might change his mind, Skunk quickly pulled him inside.

"This is fun," Skunk said as they got into their beds.

Shortly after, they fell asleep . . . but not for long.

Little Bunny was soon awakened by a terrible smell.
"What smells?" he asked as he jumped up.
"I'm afraid I do," said Skunk. "I forgot someone else
was in my room. I got scared and sprayed."
"Well, thanks for having me, but I can't sleep with
that smell!"

So Little Bunny left and hopped some more until he
reached his good friend Porcupine.

"May I sleep here tonight?"

"Certainly," said Porcupine. "You take my bed and I'll
sleep on the floor."

"Yippee!" shouted Little Bunny as he climbed into
Porcupine's bed and bounced around with excitement.

"*OUCH!*" he screamed. "What do you have in here?"

"It's just my quills," said Porcupine. "I lose some every now and then."

"Well, thanks for having me, but I can't sleep with those prickles!"

So Little Bunny left and hopped some more until he reached his good friend Bear.

"May I sleep here tonight?"

"Why sure, make yourself at home," said Bear.

By now Little Bunny was so tired he just curled up on the floor and went right to sleep.

But very soon after, Little Bunny was wakened
by a loud, rumbling noise.

Oh no, it's thundering! he thought.

But it wasn't thundering at all. His friend Bear
was snoring!

"Well, I can't sleep with that snoring!" said
Little Bunny.

So he left and hopped some more until he reached his
good friend Owl.

"May I sleep here tonight?"

"Why yes, if you want to," said Owl. "Just follow me."

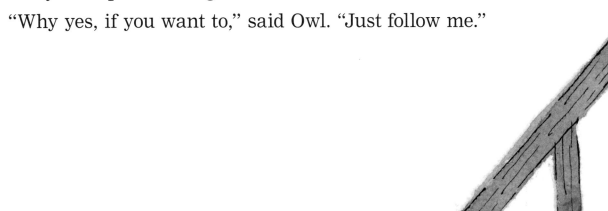

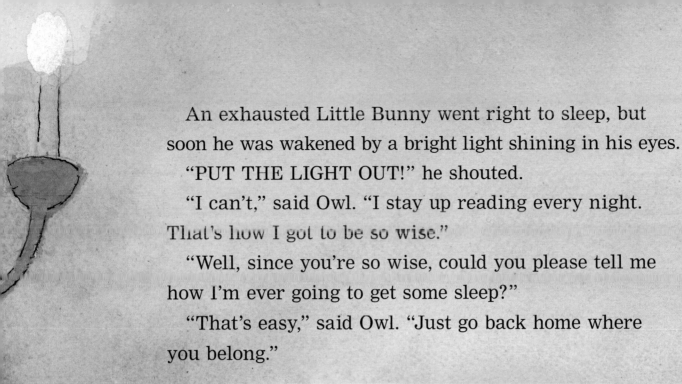

An exhausted Little Bunny went right to sleep, but soon he was wakened by a bright light shining in his eyes.

"PUT THE LIGHT OUT!" he shouted.

"I can't," said Owl. "I stay up reading every night. That's how I got to be so wise."

"Well, since you're so wise, could you please tell me how I'm ever going to get some sleep?"

"That's easy," said Owl. "Just go back home where you belong."

Little Bunny took his wise friend's advice. Too tired to hop, he dragged himself home. His bed never looked so good to him before.

He jumped right in.

"How wonderful!" he said to himself as
he snuggled down. "No crunching noise,
no terrible smell, no prickly quills, no snoring,
and no bright lights. Just me, by myself, and
peace and quiet. Now I can fall asleep!"

And that's just what Little Bunny did!